The Adventures of Lucky Cent

Children, have you ever heard that "money talks"?
Well they really do!

ePublished by Original Writing Ltd., Dublin, 2014.

Once upon a time there was a little coin called "Lucky Cent". He was a small shiny coin made of copper. He was different from all the other coins as he had a cut on his head, which he got when he was made. The cut did not bother Lucky at all as he liked being different.

Lucky came from a large family. There were eight in Lucky's family. He had three brothers, two sisters a mammy and a daddy. His brothers and sisters were all of different ages. His brothers were aged 50, 20 and 10. His sisters were aged 5 and 2. His mummy was much older. She was 100 and his daddy was even older. He was 200.

Lucky's family lived in a pretty house called "Piggy Bank" which was pink with bright yellow spots. Piggy bank belonged to a little boy called Luke. Luke was a clever boy who liked to collect coins. He collected many things like stamps, bottle tops and even buttons. But his coin collection was his favourite.

Luke had a mean brother called Eric who always tried to steal Luke's collections.
Luke locked his bedroom door to stop Eric stealing his collections.

One day Luke forgot to lock his bedroom door and while he was out playing football his mean brother Eric sneaked into his room. Eric knew Luke had a coin collection and he lifted Luke's Piggy Bank down from the shelf. Turning the piggy bank upside down Eric shook it until a coin fell out through the slot on top.

Inside Lucky Cent tried to hold onto his mother's hand but his grip was not strong enough. His hand slipped out of his mother's and he fell out through the slot into Eric's hand. Suddenly Eric heard Luke coming up the stairs so he quickly put the Piggy Bank back on the shelf. He ran out of the bedroom with Lucky Cent. Lucky's family were very sad.

Eric cycled his bike down to the corner sweet shop at the end of the street to spend Lucky Cent on sweets. The sweet shop stocked all kinds of sweets. Eric really wanted a bubble gum and he handed Lucky Cent to the shopkeeper. She then put Lucky into the till drawer and Eric left with his favourite bubble gum.

The drawer was very dark. He was scared. Suddenly he heard a voice. "Hey! Move over!". Lucky realised he wasn't alone. There were lots of coins in the drawer. They were all complaining. "Get off me! You are squashing me!".

Then Lucky heard a bell ring and the drawer opened. "Here is your change my dear!". Next thing Lucky and a few other coins were lifted out of the drawer and thrown into the purse belonging to a long haired girl.

There were different coins in her purse. They were all excited as they had been in the drawer for a long time and now finally they were moving again. One bright gold coin called "Fifty" asked Lucky "Where are you from?". "I am from Piggy Bank and I miss my Mammy and Daddy" said Lucky. "Don't worry said Fifty. I am sure you will see them again".

As they were talking they could hear loud music and could glimpse flashing lights from above. Some of the coins became excited. "I know this place. I was here before. This place is amazing" said Fifty. "They call it Leisureland" he said with excitement. Suddenly the purse was opened wider and Lucky was lifted up high in the air. He looked down and could see the other coins in the purse. The long haired girl pushed him into a slot on top of a large shiny machine.

Lucky rolled down a short slide and then bumped over and back crashing suddenly as he fell down into the machine. Finally he landed on a flat surface that seemed to be moving in and out. Lucky tried to hold on to the wall but the floor was sliding over and back too fast. Next thing he fell flat and found himself being pushed in amongst hundreds of other coins all lying on their backs.

There was no room on the shelf for Lucky and so a few of the other coins fell off the shelf when Lucky was pushed in. The coins that fell shouted for joy. "Yippee were free!" they shouted. This seemed very strange to Lucky. The other coins asked: "Whats your name?". "Lucky" he said. "Well, Lucky, I hope you bring us luck. We have been in here for weeks".

Lucky looked around and he saw lots oft coins. He never knew there could be so many. Some were shiny new and some were dirty. The flashing lights made it hard to see and the music was very loud. "What a strange place this is", he thought to himself. Next thing, a big burly man with grey hair opened the machine and using a small shovel he scooped up Lucky and lots of his new companions. He poured them carelessly into a bucket on the floor.

But Lucky missed the bucket and he fell onto the floor and rolled around for ages and ages. The machine man didn't notice that Lucky had not gone into the bucket. Lucky rolled to the end of the room and stopped where he hit the wall. His head was spinning and he felt quite dizzy, but he was unhurt since he was made of metal.

After a while he looked up and could see a brother and sister arguing. "It's your turn to pay for the pool game" said the boy. "No it's your turn" said the girl. "Don't be so miserable and spend a penny now and again!" shouted the boy. At this, the girl reluctantly took a coin out of her pocket and placed it into the machine. "There I hope your'e happy !" she shouted. Just then she noticed Lucky Cent under the pool table. She reached down and picked him up. "Ha ha! This must be my lucky penny" she cried.

She opened her purse and dropped him in. He landed beside the other coins who were all very pale and sad. They had not seen daylight for many years. They wondered where Lucky had come from. "We have been in here for years. We never get to go anywhere" they cried. Lucky was very depressed. He missed his mammy and daddy all the more now. He began to wonder if he would ever see them again.

Suddenly they heard a gruff voice, "Give me all your money or else". The miserable girl was being robbed by a thief with a mask over his face. In floods of tears she opened her pocket and gave him all her coins. Lucky was dropped into a bag with all the other coins.

The thief ran off and Lucky was shaken and tossed around with all the other coins in the bag. Eventually the bag stopped shaking and all the coins were emptied out onto a desk in front of a scary man in a pinstriped suit called Mr. Greco. He had a black moustache and big black eyebrows. Mr. Greco looked at Lucky " My, my what have we got here a funny little fellow with a cut in his head!" Lucky was trembling and quite terrified. Mr. Greco began to stack all the coins one on top of the other in neat little piles. Then he began counting them.

When he was finished he put the same coin types together in separate little plastic bags. Lucky was very scared. Then Mr Greco lifted all of the bags and walked across the street to a large building called "The Bank".

He walked up to the counter and handed all of the bags over to the lady. She emptied out all of the coins and put each of the coins in neat little trays. Lucky was amazed at all the different coins in the Bank. There were coins from all over the world with strange accents. There were American coins, English coins, Russian coins and even Australian coins. It was like a coin airport.

The Russian coin looked over at Lucky – "Allo leetle fellow, why ave you got a cut on ze ead"? he said. Lucky replied "I don't know, I'm different". "Don't mind him mate," said the Australian coin and the English coin said "Oh, stop fussing you lot and leave the new boy alone!" Lucky was amazed at all these funny coins. Just as Lucky had given up all hope of ever seeing his family again he heard his owner's voice – "Could I change this coin for 1 cent coins please?" It was Luke. Upon hearing this Lucky was lifted from the tray and found himself back in Luke's hand once again.

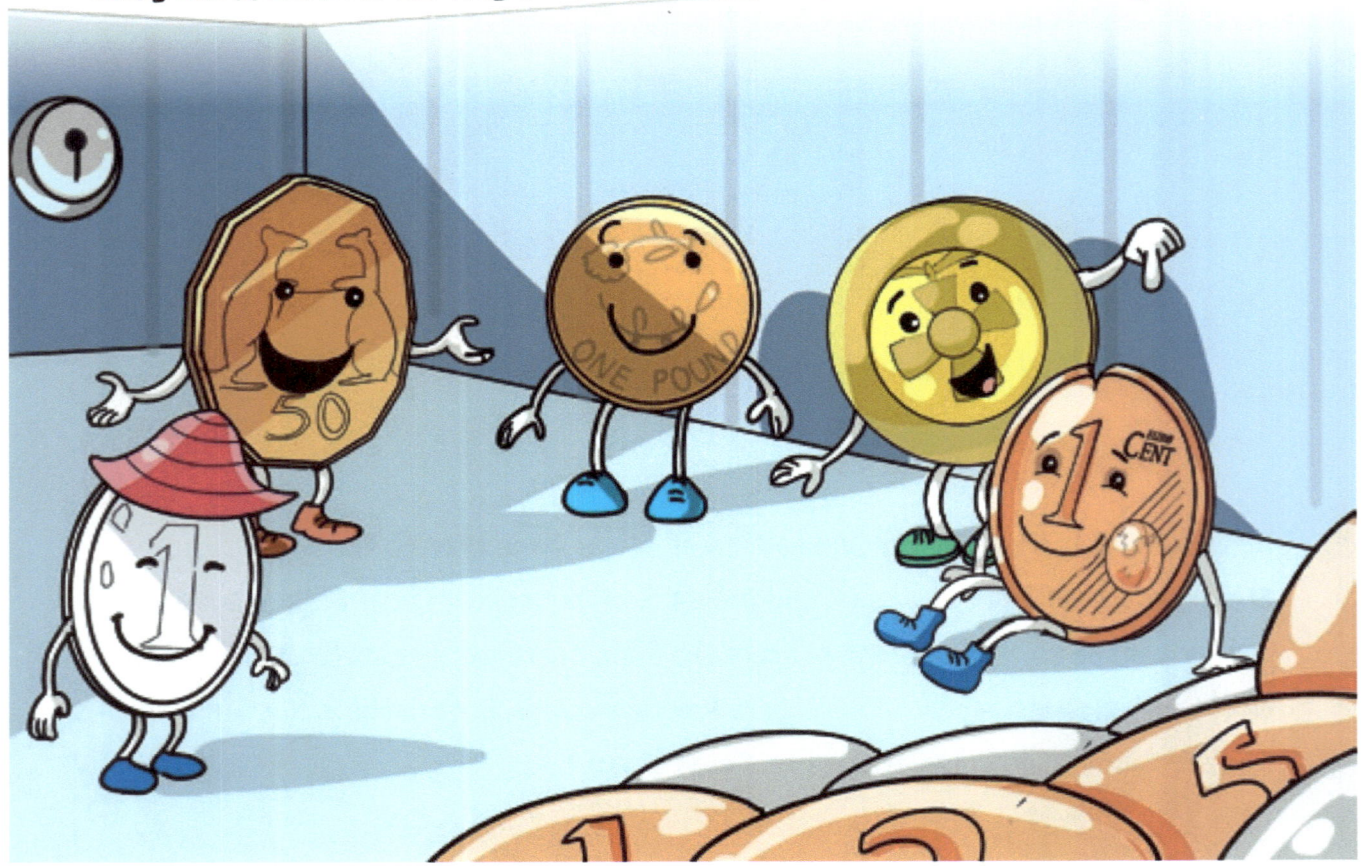

Lucky was delighted and Luke was surprised. Luke had come into the bank to get a new coin for his collection. When the lady handed him the coin Luke saw it was his Lucky cent as he had a cut on his head. He was over the moon and ran all the way home to tell everyone. He put Lucky back into the piggy bank to be with his family again. Lucky sighed and put his head down and fell fast asleep.

He was glad to be home after his big adventure. Everything was quiet in Piggy Bank at last.

www.ingramcontent.com/pod-product-compliance
Lightning Source LLC
Chambersburg PA
CBHW041544240626